THE MOOD OF NATURE

Gaurav Ghosh

ISBN 978-93-5667-984-9
© Gaurav Ghosh 2023

Published in India 2023 by Pencil

A brand of

One Point Six Technologies Pvt. Ltd.
Unit no. 26, Ground Floor, Building A1,
Wadala Truck Terminal Road,
Near Post Office, Antop Hill, Mumbai - 400037
E connect@thepencilapp.com
W www.thepencilapp.com

Author biography

Unveiling the Inspiring Journey of Gaurav Ghosh: A Rising Star in the Literary World

Introduction: Meet Gaurav Ghosh, A Talented Student with a Passion for Writing

Gaurav Ghosh biography, Gaurav Ghosh writer, student author, young author, study at Netarhat Residential School a class 9th student

The Genesis of a Dream: How Gaurav Found Inspiration in the Depths of Knowledge

Netarhat Residential School library, finding ideas from books, source of inspiration for writing, the role of family support in writing career

A First Step Towards Success: The Debut Book that Showcases Gaurav's Unique Voice

Gaurav Ghosh's first book The mood of nature , literary debut at a young age, narrative style and themes explored in the book

The Power of Family Support: How Gaurav's Loved Ones Believed in His Potential and Encouraged His Writing Journey

Role of family support for young writers, parents' encouragement in pursuing creative passions at an early age

His father - Nimai chandra Ghosh

His mother - Bhawani Ghosh

and he says that he get a special support by his

Maternal uncle (mama) - SUJIT KUMAR SARKAR

Nurturing Creativity at Netarhat Residential School Library: The Wellspring of Ideas and Knowledge

Netarhat Residential School library contributions to Gaurav's writing journey; access to diverse literature and resources;

Paving the Way for Future Success: The Bright Road Ahead for Gaurav Ghosh and His Writing Career

Growth prospects for young authors; potential future works by Gaurav; aspirations and goals as a budding writer;

Whether you're seeking inspiration from his journey or looking for an insight into the world of young talents,

Gaurav Ghosh's incredible debut is a testimony to the power of passion and family support. Don't miss out on this rising star in the literary world!

CONTENTS

Acknowledgements

In this section, we extend our heartfelt gratitude and acknowledgements to the people who have played a significant role in the creation and publication of this book. As the author, it is essential for me to express my deepest appreciation to those who have supported and encouraged me throughout this journey.

Firstly, I would like to express my immense gratitude to my friends and family. Their unwavering support, constructive criticism, and belief in my abilities have been invaluable. They have been a constant source of inspiration and motivation throughout the writing process.

A special mention goes out to the parents without whose love, guidance, and encouragement this book would not have been possible. Their endless support has nurtured my passion for writing from an early age, and I am forever grateful for their unwavering belief in me.

I would also like to extend a sincere thank you to the librarian of Netarhat Residential School. Rajesh Raman ji. The access to an extensive collection of books provided by the library has broadened my horizons as a writer. The knowledge gained from those books has enabled me to shape my ideas more effectively.

Lastly, but certainly not least, I want to acknowledge all those individuals who contributed their time, expertise or insights during research for this book. Their valuable input has enriched its content immensely.

To everyone mentioned above and countless others who have supported me silently behind the scenes: your love, critiques, encouragement,and contributions are greatly appreciated. Thank you all for being part of this incredible journey towards bringing this book into existence.

—

In my book "The Mood of Nature: How Nature Combines Us," I take inspiration from netarhat residential school we embark on a journey to explore the profound connection between humanity and the natural world. This captivating book takes us through a thought-provoking exploration of how nature intertwines with every aspect of our lives, shaping our emotions

Introduction

In my book "The Mood of Nature: How Nature Combines Us," I take inspiration from netarhat residential school we embark on a journey to explore the profound connection between humanity and the natural world. This captivating book takes us through a thought-provoking exploration of how nature intertwines with every aspect of our lives, shaping our emotions, thoughts, and actions.

Nature has always been an intrinsic part of human existence, providing solace in times of distress and inspiration in moments of creativity. By immersing ourselves in nature's wonders, we discover a profound sense of tranquility and find ourselves deeply connected to something much greater than ourselves.

Throughout this book, we delve into the ways nature has nurtured our souls throughout history. We uncover the mysteries behind how gazing at a starlit sky sparks awe and wonder within us or how walking barefoot on lush green grass can instantly rejuvenate both body and mind.

As we turn each page, we encounter stories from individuals whose lives have been forever changed by their encounters with nature. From mountaintop adventures to tranquil walks along sandy shores, their experiences illuminate the transformative power that lies within our natural surroundings.

"The Mood of Nature: How Nature Combines Us" brings together scientific research, philosophical insights, and personal narratives to present a compelling case for embracing nature as an integral part of our daily lives. Through this exploration, we gain valuable understanding about not only how nature impacts us but also how we can reciprocate its care by becoming stewards for a more harmonious world.

Prepare to be captivated by this eloquent exploration into the mood-altering effects that accompany our connection with nature. Whether you are an avid explorer or simply long for moments of serenity amidst your busy life, "The Mood of Nature" promises to illuminate the incredible bond that exists between humanity and the natural world.

The beauty of beach

The sun was just beginning to peek up above the horizon, casting its soft orange and pink hue across the stunning beach landscape. Emily took a deep breath of the salt air and felt the tension begin to leave her body—she was home.

The beach was always so beautiful this time of day—the lapping waves of the mystic ocean mindlessly cradling the craggy rocks and the rolling sand dunes had a peaceful quality that soothed Emily's soul. She stood there, captivated by the beauty of it all, and with a deep sigh, she decided to take a walk along the shore.

The sand was cool and soft beneath Emily's bare feet, and she couldn't help but smile as she walked. Her eyes scanned the horizon, admiring the wild and untamed beauty of nature and taking in the sight of the sky slowly transitioning into that bright, vibrant blue.

Coming around the bend, she could now see the rugged cliffs that surrounded the beach. Shaped by the wind and the waves, these cliffs gave off an aura of strength and power, as if they had been here since the dawn of time and perhaps even longer.

Reaching the water's edge, she couldn't imagine a place more grand or more beautiful. The waves seemed alive, with each one pushing forward and crashing against the shore like a living creature. The colors were stunning—from deep blues and aquamarines to the lighter shades of green and teal.

Emily couldn't help but be amazed at the power of nature as she watched the waves crash against the rocks and sand. It was a humbling moment to be reminded of just how powerful nature could be, and yet how delicate and fragile it was too.

Standing there, mesmerized by the beautiful beach landscape, Emily felt something release inside her—she felt content and grateful for this moment of peace and beauty. She realized that in today's busy world, it was easy to feel overwhelmed, but here, on the beach, all that was forgotten and she was filled with a sense of wonder and awe.

As the sun slowly began to set, Emily turned and slowly began to make her way back. Before she knew it, the beach faded into the horizon and she was left with the memory of this beautiful landscape still imprinted in her mind.

The distance towards the hill station

As the bus sluggishly made its way up the winding roads of the mountain, the terrain became steeper and more rugged. Its tires intermittently screeching on the gravel road as if to remind its passengers that the ascension was far from complete. Inside the bus, the atmosphere was cozy and the occupants of the vehicle were eagerly anticipatory of what awaited them at the top.

In the distance, a light fluff of snow-white clouds seemed to be perched on the peaks of the mountain, lending an air of mysterious beauty to whatever lay ahead. As the passengers watched the clouds dance about in the wind, they felt a calmness come over them that they hadn't felt in months. After what seemed like an eternity, they had arrived at their destination.

As they stepped off the bus, they were hit with a wave of cold air that enveloped their senses and stirred up long forgotten dreams and memories from deep within. They were met with rows of alpine trees adorned with thick blankets of snow, which almost looked like they had been wrapped in white cotton. Everywhere was blissfully peaceful and beautiful as the snow fluttered gently through the air.

The travelers looked around in awe at the stunning landscape and their spirits were lifted by what they saw. Even the cold air seemed to have a lightening effect and they could feel their worries dissipating as they took in their surroundings.

The travelers waded through the powdery white snow, leaving behind trails of footprints among the trees. They slowly made their way to the village at the top of the hill, feeling the warmth of the sun as they basked in the beauty of the snow-covered landscape.

When they reached the top, they were met with a village full of life. People were outside enjoying the snow and more were safely tucked away in their homes, enjoying the warmth and safe haven the village provided against the cold winter months.

The travelers stayed at the village for a few days, reveling in the beauty and tranquility of the hill station. During their stay, they sampled local cuisine, hiked among the alpine trees, and explored the winding streets of the village. At night, the stars glowed a brilliant white, adding to the serenity of the village.

The travelers were hesitant to leave, but eventually they had to bid farewell to the village and their peaceful, snow-covered hill station home. With much reluctance they hopped back onto the bus and as it started its descent down the mountain, they looked back with admiration, feeling as if they had been away from home for much longer than a few days.

Although it was the end of their stay, it was also the beginning of a newfound love for the hill station they had visited. They found solace and beauty in its vastness and even in the cold weather, they felt a warmth inside their hearts. As they drove away, they were forever grateful for the moments they had spent at the beautiful hill station, where the nature fell a snow like white cotton.

We and nature

Once upon a time in a far away land, there was a bucolic town where human and nature formed an everlasting bond. This bond was so special that the residents of the town would often take a pause in their day-to-day lives to appreciate and honor what nature had to offer.

Far beyond the town's borders was a magnificent forest, lush and green. It was filled with all manner of trees and plants, some of which could be found nowhere else in the land. Every night, the townspeople took time to walk among the trees, feeling peaceful and rejuvenated by the natural environment.

The relationship between human and nature was always mutual. The townspeople never forgot to take only what they needed, and gave back what they could in return. They shared whatever surplus they had with the forest and its inhabitants, giving back to the environment what had been graciously bestowed upon them.

One day, a great storm destroyed much of the forest. The trees were uprooted and the sky was blocked by thick clouds of smoke and dust. Much of the land looked like an endless, barren wasteland.

The townspeople were devastated by the destruction they witnessed, but they were determined not to give up. They worked hard to restore life to the devastated forest. The townspeople planted trees, dug out rivers, and spread topsoil to help the environment to heal. As the townspeople worked, they formed a bond that was deeper and more meaningful than ever before.

The forest slowly but surely returned to its former glory, aided by the townspeople's dedication. Animals returned to the land and the trees flourished once more.

For many years, the townspeople and the nature stayed in strong partnership. The residents always respected and thanked the environment for its bounty, and the environment provided the necessary nourishment and care for the people to thrive.

The strong bond between human and nature grew and flourished throughout the generations. Each new generation of the townspeople passed on the lesson of gratitude and respect for nature to the next. The forest was a reminder of the power that humans have to nurture the land and gain the joy and benefits of living in harmony with the environment.

The strong love between human and nature could be felt to this day, and the townspeople awoke each day with a greater appreciation for the beauty and bounty of nature in their lives.

Life with nature

Irina stared out the window, lost in dreams of faraway places. She had grown up in the small town of Waterstone, a town shrouded in mystery. People rarely ventured outside its borders, scared of the unknown and the adventures that they could come across. The town was safe, though, and residents all seemed content with their daily routines- the same shops to visit, the same people to see, the same roads to wind through on the way to and from errands.

But Irina could not be content here; it felt too safe, too predictable. She wanted an adventure. She wanted to explore the world and experience new things. She wanted to know what lay beyond those distant horizons.

One night, she decided to take a chance and follow her dreams. She packed her bags, said goodbye to her family and friends, and set out on her own. She traveled for months, seeing new places, trying new things, and having new experiences. She was able to stay in touch with the people she left behind through letters and paid visits whenever possible.

Time flew by and soon Irina had been living away from home for a year. She had, in that time, seen so much of the world and met so many new and interesting people. In a way, it was like she had lived a thousand lives in one lifetime.

At the end of her journey, Irina had come full circle and was back in Waterstone. But this time she was different. She was aware and grateful of all that the world had to offer. And although she was still scared of the unknown, she was now more confident in her ability to take on new adventures and experiences.

Irina now lived every day to the fullest, both in and out of Waterstone. Her perspective had changed dramatically, and she was now willing to take on any challenge that came her way. Her friends no longer understood what had changed in her, but they were glad to see the same friend living within her, albeit with an extra layer of self-confidence.

Although many years would pass, Irina never forgot the adventures she had experienced. And she always looked back on them and thought of how different her life would have been had she not taken that first step. In living a thousand lives in one year, she had only needed a single leap of faith.

Nature war with nature

It was a peaceful morning in the land of the green meadows and majestic mountains, a place few knew about and even fewer reached. Here, nature's beauty was not lost to the concrete jungles of civilization. The sun's emerald rays shone on the rolling hills, dazzling in its splendor. The birds chirped their joyous melodies and the creatures of the wild scampered about the woodlands in search of sustenance.

But soon, all the peace and harmony of the land was shattered with the distant rumbling of war. Heeding the call of the drums, thousands upon thousands of armed soldiers assembled in the meadows. They had come to wage a war for the land and all its jewels of nature.

Leading the army was a cruel and ruthless leader who wanted to gain complete control over the land and all its resources. He was determined to transform the green meadows into a kingdom of death and destruction as he waged an all out war against nature. The rich soils and lush mountains were to become nothing but his battlefields in his ultimate quest for power.

For weeks the fighting raged on with no end in sight. Everywhere the soldiers marched, the birds were driven away, and the creatures of the wild took refuge in their homes. Plants were crushed and the air was polluted with the smell of death. Nature had been forced into poverty, its once bountiful resources pillaged and plundered.

The war was not without its heroes, however. Some brave and righteous souls took it upon themselves to stand up against the oppressors and protect nature and its wildlife. Armed with nothing but passion and courage, they fought for days without rest to preserve the land and all its beauty.

In the end, the defenders of nature emerged victorious. The oppressor had been vanquished and the meadows and mountains were returned to the way they were before the war. Nature was allowed to flourish again and the birds returned to sing their joyful songs once more.

The war was now over, but its lesson was learned. It was a reminder that nature should never be taken for granted, and that we must fight to protect it, lest we lose to those who seek to tear it apart.

The destructive nature

The sun beat down relentlessly on the small village on the edge of the great forest. It had been a thriving place, surrounded by lush vegetation that supported its inhabitants.

But now the once verdant landscape was nothing more than empty stretches of dirt. The trees, the vegetation, and the wild animals had all been wiped out by rampant deforestation.

The villagers who had once made their livelihoods in the forest had been left destitute and desperate. Not only had their livelihood been lost, but they had also been disconnected from the land that had been their home for generations.

The effects of the destruction were widespread. The air was heavy with dust and pollution. The earth was barren and lifeless. The birds no longer sang their songs over the treetops.

But the most tragic consequence of the deforestation was the deep anguish the villagers felt in their hearts. For logging had not only destroyed the beauty and bounty of the forest, it had also destroyed the very soul of the village.

Despite these difficult times, the villagers still clung onto hope and vowed that one day, they would rebuild the land and restore the forest to its once majestic beauty. But until that day came, the destruction of nature in the village would linger in the memories of all who had witnessed it firsthand

life changing goddess

The sun shone brightly in the afternoon sky, reflecting across the emptied valley below. All of the land was devoid of vibrant green trees, not a leaf in sight. The sun was the only sign of life amidst the arid and cracked dirt.

The man stood alone in the middle of the valley, taking in the vast emptiness and feeling a pang of sadness in his heart. He had lost everything in life. He had lost a job, his marriage, his home, and was dispossessed of all that he had loved. He felt lost and overwhelmed with sadness as he looked at the terrain around him.

Trying to fight off the sadness, the man began to wander aimlessly through the valley, barely registering where he was stepping. Eventually, he reached the dried-up river bed that cuts through the valley. He was mesmerized by the sound of the wind blowing seductively through the river.

The man sat down next to the river and proceeded to empty his pockets, carefully counting out all of his money. When he was done, he had a paltry sum of $47.

What am I going to do with this, he asked himself. I have nothing and no one left to turn to.

At that moment, something snapped inside him. His tragic situation, coupled with the tranquil beauty of the valley, stirred something deep within him, something ancient and wise. He knew what he had to do.

He began by collecting small rocks from the banks of the river bed. He worked meticulously and with purpose, collecting each rock with admiration and respect. After collecting the stones, he walked out of the valley and purchased some soil and small saplings.

For days on end, the man worked diligently in the valley. He replanted the riverbed with thousands of saplings, carefully watering each one everyday in order to keep them healthy and alive. That $47 bought him enough saplings to fill the valley with life.

As if by magic, as the man planted more trees, life began to come back into the valley. Eventually, the entire valley was teeming with life - beautiful trees and flowers growing every single day.

The man stood in the center of the valley and watched enviously as the life around him flourished and grew. He wasn't sure what he had done, but it seemed to be working.

As the months passed, the man found himself feeling happy again. He had planted and nurtured the trees, and in exchange the trees had nurtured him. Eventually, he was able to get back on his feet and start a new job and even form a new relationship. He felt like he had been given a second chance at life, and he was determined to make the most of it.

Years later, the man returned to the valley and marveled at the incredible transformation that had taken place. Trees and plants of all sizes and colors lined the banks of the river, birds sang joyfully in the branches and life thrived in the valley.

The man smiled to himself and was filled with joy and peace. He had recovered from his loss through the power and beauty of nature, and he was humbled and thankful for this gift of life. He stood in the valley and was thankful for the wonderful life he had been given.

Nature as Mother

The trees rustled in the wind, their large branches swaying in the air while their leaves blew about. Emily took in the tranquil scenery, marveling at its beauty. On either side of her, tall trunks swirled up the sides of the mountain, the gentle rising line of evergreen trees filling the horizon.

She closed her eyes and inhaled deeply, enjoying the clean smell of the fresh air around her. Although the atmosphere had a chill, Emily could feel the warmth of the sun on her face. The air felt so alive that it could be called a living being.

It was then it hit her; as she stood amidst nature, she felt a profound sense of peace. She knew that she was part of this natural order. The trees that reached their branches skyward might have been bigger than her, but she was no less a part of their existence.

At that moment, she was aware of a deep connection with all things living and the distant voices that seemed to quiet her in her hour of need.

A bird flew across her path, singing a beautiful song of joy and celebration. Emily smiled through her tears, knowing that the bird was not just any old singer, but rather nature singing its own tune. Then, a gust of wind settled her hair and rippled across her face, clearing away the sorrow that had consumed her.

Slowly, the peculiar sensation began to take on a more human shape. In that moment, Emily felt as if the trees and wind and birds had come together to form a new being—a new mother. A mother of nature, who was far-reaching and powerful enough to support the sky, yet gentle enough to caress her face in the way only a mother's love could.

It didn't feel like a god-like figure; instead, it felt more like a friend. A friend who was always there to comfort her and guide her through life's winding pathways. Nature, she would learn, was a loyal and faithful ally, one who understood life's sorrows and celebrated its joys with her.

Yes, this was nature as a mother. Emily smiled. Her heart was full, and she realized with a newfound appreciation of her place in the world. She had finally found her true home and the one place where she could always find solace—among the trees, birds, and wind, in the arms of her ever-loving mother—Nature.

Nature works depend on you

Nature like a bullet can shred and tear,
Offering destruction, chaos, and fear.
Like a wave in the sea that crashes the shore,
Nature brings force that we can't ignore.

Yet Nature can also be a savior to us,
Like a mother's embrace in a rush of warm fuzz,
Whether it be the rain that nourishes plants,
Or the sun that gives us all of its might and grants.

Nature gives and takes, as this is its role.
Depend upon it, respecting its soul.
It helps to sustain us, and ground us and more.
Nature the bearer of new life and lore.

If there is any writing mistake take place so please don't mind
This is my first book
Anf if any suggestions contact me
Email- gghoshjmt01@gmail.com

Love nature

writing

Table of Contents:

Introduction

1. The Power of Nature

2. Connecting with Nature

3. Nature and Mental Health

4. Restoring Nature

5. Exploring Nature

Conclusion

Introduction

Nature is a wonderful thing; it's infinitely powerful and undeniably healing. From its vast oceans and lush forests, majestic mountains and peaceful meadows, to its countless stars and twinkling fireflies, it inspires and nurtures us to take a step back from our everyday lives and appreciate the world around us. It's easy to take nature for granted, but when we embrace it with open arms, we can experience its full power and beauty.

Love Nature is a step-by-step guide for reconnecting with nature for a healthier, happier life. It dives into the power of nature, how to truly connect with it, and how it impacts mental health. It examines the importance of restoring nature and the wonderful feeling of exploring it, showing us that nature is our teacher, healer, and friend.

1. The Power of Nature

As humans, we often forget just how powerful nature is. Whether it's serenely staring at stars, standing at the top of a mountain, or taking a dip in a crystal clear lake, there's something special about immersing ourselves in nature. It offers a wonderful sense of peace and can help to heal physical and emotional wounds, restore balance, and boost creativity.

But its power goes well beyond providing comfort and joy. Nature is an essential part of our lives, with its importance in sustaining our physical health, mental wellbeing, and even our economic stability. Its beauty is essential for our health and wellbeing, both physically and mentally. The power of nature and its beauty must be treasured and respected.

2. Connecting with Nature

The first step to truly connecting with nature is to understand its power and beauty. To connect with its essence, we must take the time to appreciate, meditate on, and be reminded of its greatness. To do this we need to be mindful of our surroundings and find ways to make time to explore, relax in, and just be in nature. It's also important to not forget the little things that make nature so special, like watching the birds fly through the sky and listening to the leaves rustle in the wind.

But it goes beyond just admiring the beauty; we must also understand the importance of caring for it. Taking care of nature is a responsible and rewarding act, as it ensures its continued existence and allows us to enjoy it for years to come. To truly understand and appreciate nature, we must develop a sense of respect and responsibility towards it.

3. Nature and Mental Health

Nature is essential for our mental health. Taking time to relax in nature can help to reduce stress, anxiety, and depression. The natural environment has healing powers and time spent in nature can be a powerful way to boost mood, focus, and creativity. It's not just the scenery that helps in this regard, but also the sounds and smells of nature.

Spending time in nature can also be an effective way to relieve loneliness. Connecting with nature allows us to engage with something bigger than ourselves and appreciate the beauty of life. It can be a wonderful way to cultivate self-love and acceptance, and can be a powerful motivator to put time into improving our lives and the world around us.

4. Restoring Nature

Restoring nature is another important aspect of loving nature. From deforestation and pollution, to climate change and species extinction, many of our actions have had a negative impact on the environment. So it's up to us to show nature that we care by taking steps to restore it.

This includes planting trees and plants, conserving energy, reducing waste, recycling, and supporting sustainable practices like organic agriculture. It's also important to protect wildlife and learn more about the plants and creatures that live in our local area. Although restoring nature might seem like a small gesture, it can lead to big change over time, and it all starts with us.

5. Exploring Nature

Exploring nature is one of the best ways to experience its immense power and beauty. From hikes in the mountains to picnics in the park, exploring nature in all its forms can be a wonderful way to recharge and enjoy life. It also offers plenty of opportunities for adventure, like traveling to remote destinations, scuba diving, or learning more about indigenous cultures.

Going on nature trips doesn't have to be expensive or complicated; simple activities like camping, star gazing, and bird watching can be just as rewarding. Exploring nature can provide us with valuable lessons, whether we learn something new about ourselves or gain a greater appreciation for our planet.

Conclusion

Ultimately, learning to love nature is all about finding ways to connect with and appreciate its power and beauty. Whether it's taking time to appreciate its beauty, caring for it, or exploring

Work for nature

drive

Like many of us this year, Mother Nature has endured a difficult and trying time. Despite the chaos surrounding us, life still moves on, and nature is no different. With natural disasters increasing in frequency and intensity due to climate change, nature needs all the help it can get.

That's why a group of passionate environmentalists and conservationists have organized a new type of event – a 'Nature Blood Drive'.

The goal of the Nature Blood Drive is to inspire individuals to take action for nature. In exchange for a small donation, participants can receive symbolic gifts – like packets of wildflower seeds or small saplings – to plant. The saplings and wildflowers will help rebuild and regenerate forests and natural habitats in depleted areas.

But the Nature Blood Drive isn't just about donations; it's also about getting people more involved in nature conservation. Participants can sign up to volunteer with the local conservationists for reforestation projects, beach clean-ups, or habitat restoration.

The Nature Blood Drive is a unique way to make real change for nature. So if you're looking for ways to help our planet, why not join the Nature Blood Drive? Every little bit helps, and together, we can make a difference.

Nature also Cry

The morning sun shone through the treetops, as if the sky was smiling. It was perfect weather, soothing and peaceful; it felt as if the whole world was at ease. The birds were singing, the squirrels were scurrying around, and the flowers swayed in the light breeze. It seemed like a perfect day – until the tears appeared in the sky.

The clouds darkened, as if the blue canopy of the sky was crying tears of sorrow. It seemed like nature itself was sad, and soon the tears started pouring down. Soon, the ground was flooded with water, and all the birds, squirrels and flowers were submerged beneath the rising waters.

The humans watched helplessly, not knowing what to do. The relentless tears of sorrow weren't stopping anytime soon, and soon the entire landscape was submerged in the water. It seemed too late for the humans to save nature, and so all they could do was stand, helpless, and watch nature cry.

The people tried their best to help the animal and plants, but the water kept flooding, and soon all they could do was mourn for the beauty that had been taken away by the tears of sorrow. Nature had been robbed, and the people stood, teary-eyed, wishing they could have done something to protect it.

After a while, the rain stopped, and the sun started to shine once again. When the waters receded, the people saw a tragedy of destruction - the trees, the animals and the plants all gone, swept away by the tears of sorrow.

The people never knew what caused nature to cry that day. But, it was a tearful reminder to the people to take care of our planet and not to take it for granted. Nature had shown us that sometimes, even the strongest of beings need a shoulder to lean on.

A war with plastic

Nature had seen enough. For too long, humans had polluted and destroyed her lands, contaminating the waters and air with their disgusting creations. Plastic had become the biggest enemy, polluting the land, poisoning the animals, and choking the trees. Nature knew she had to protect her home, and so, with a gust of wind, she summoned her army of trees, plants, and animals to wage war against the intruders.

The plastic erupted from the ground, overwhelming the forests and grasslands alike. Rivers and streams were filled with its foul smell, and the air was thick with its toxicity. Nature and her army stood firm in the face of enemy forces. The trees clawed and scraped at the plastic, tearing it apart with their roots, while the animals attacked it with their claws and bite. The plants sent their long tendrils into the plastic evil, choking and smothering it.

Meanwhile, the humans began to take notice of the fight. Ignoring Nature's warnings and pleas to stop the destruction, they marched onward, creating even more plastic to add to their mountains of waste.

For weeks the battle waged, neither side relenting. Nature and her army fought with everything they had, but the humans just kept creating more, their greed and destruction unending. Finally, when the trees had been reduced to bare trunks, the animals exhausted, and the plants wilting in the polluted air, Nature called on her final ally - the weather.

A powerful storm roared in, obliterating the plastic and washing it back to the ocean from whence it came. The rains and winds cleansed the land, and Nature and her army emerged victorious.

From that day forward, Nature has protected her lands from the pollution of humans, reminding us all that Nature always wins in a fight between two worlds.

www.ingramcontent.com/pod-product-compliance
Lightning Source LLC
La Vergne TN
LVHW041442170726
843492LV00008B/2770